Toads
and
Diamonds

Retold by CHARLOTTE HUCK
Pictures by
ANITA LOBEL

Greenwillow Books, New York

For Charrie and Jeannie,
both kind sisters and good friends

Watercolor and gouache paints were used for the full-color art.
The text type is Bernhard Modern.
Text copyright © 1996 by Charlotte S. Huck, Trustee of
The Charlotte S. Huck Living Trust, dated October 22, 1992
Illustrations copyright © 1996 by Anita Lobel

Greenwillow Books, a division of William Morrow & Company, Inc.,
1350 Avenue of the Americas, New York, NY 10019.
Printed in Singapore by Tien Wah Press
First Edition 10 9 8 7 6 5 4 3 2 1

Library of Congress Cataloging-in-Publication Data

Huck, Charlotte S.
Toads and diamonds / retold by Charlotte Huck ;
pictures by Anita Lobel.
Summary: Two stepsisters receive appropriate gifts
for their actions: one's words are accompanied by
flowers and jewels, the other's by toads and snakes.
ISBN 0-688-13680-X (trade)
ISBN 0-688-13681-8 (lib. bdg.)
[1. Fairy tales.   2. Folklore—France.]
I. Lobel, Anita, ill.   II. Title
PZ8.H862To   1996   398.2'094402—dc20
94-27292   CIP   AC

There once was a widow who had a daughter, Francine, and a stepdaughter, Renée. Francine was as haughty and demanding as her mother. Renée, on the other hand, had the kind disposition of her real mother, who had died when her daughter was still a child. Both her stepmother and stepsister mistreated Renée. She was forced to eat in the kitchen after cooking and serving them meals. She had to weed the vegetable garden, milk the goats, and twice a day, carrying a large pitcher, walk about a mile and a half to a spring for water.

But Renée looked forward to her walks to the spring. They were her escape from the constant demands of her stepsister and stepmother.

One day the sky was so blue, the clouds so white, and the blossoms so pink that Renée sang as she walked along. She carried some bread in her pocket to feed the birds and the rabbits. One bird flew to her shoulder to peck at the food she gave it. And she had nearly tamed a rabbit to eat from her hands.

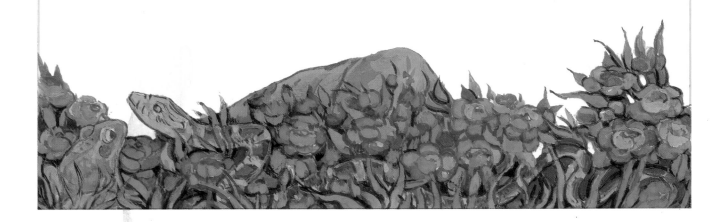

As Renée drew close to the spring, she saw an old peasant woman sitting on a rock. The old woman asked her if she would mind bringing her a drink from the spring.

"Gladly," Renée replied. Taking a cup from a pocket in her apron, she filled it with fresh spring water and gave it to the old woman.

The old woman thanked her and said, "Because you are as kind as you are beautiful, I have a gift for you. For every word you speak, a flower or a jewel will drop from your lips. And this will happen as long as there will be a need for it."

When Renée returned home, she was scolded by her stepmother for taking so long.

"I am sorry, Mother," she replied. "I stopped to help an old woman." When she spoke these words, two roses, two diamonds, and some pearls fell from her lips.

"What is this, my daughter? Diamonds and pearls are dropping from your mouth!" This was the first time her stepmother had ever called her "daughter."

Renée was so pleased that she told her everything that had happened at the spring. And as she spoke, the flowers and jewels continued to flow from her mouth.

"Francine," the astonished stepmother said, "look what comes from Renée's mouth when she speaks. You, too, can have such treasures. All you have to do is go to the spring and give the old peasant woman who sits there a drink of water."

"You'll not catch me fetching water for a peasant woman. Let Renée do so if she wants, but I'm not waiting on some old woman like a servant."

"You will go, and you will go now," ordered her mother, and she pushed Francine toward the door.

"Oh, all right. But if I have to go, I'm not carrying that heavy pitcher." She picked up her mother's silver wedding pitcher that was never taken to the spring and flounced out of the house.

Francine muttered to herself as she started down the path. Where had her sister really gotten those jewels? Surely it was just some made-up story she had told her mother.

About halfway to the spring a bird startled her by landing on her shoulder. "Here, get off me, you pesky thing," Francine said, and roughly pushed it away.

Then she spied a rabbit that came close. "H-m-m, you'd make a good stew," she said, and lunged at the rabbit, catching it by its hind leg. The rabbit squealed so loudly that it frightened her, and she let it go. It fled away into the bushes, and Francine went on her way, grumbling.

Soon she came to the spring. A beautiful young lady in a magnificent rainbow-colored dress came limping out of the woods and sat down on the rock. "I seem to have hurt my foot," she said. "Would you be so kind as to bring me some water from the spring?"

"Who do you think I am, your servant?" snapped Francine. "I don't know you. Just hobble down to the spring yourself and get your own water."

"What a rude girl," said the lady. "But I have a gift for you, anyway."

At the mention of a gift Francine looked at her and said, "I thought it was the old woman who gave gifts."

"Ah," replied the beautiful lady, "but I am the old woman, and the bird you hit, and the rabbit you hurt when you grabbed it by the leg. I do give gifts, and I have a special one for you. For every word you speak, a toad or a snake will fall from your lips. And this will happen as long as there will be a need for it."

Francine was so furious that she filled the silver pitcher to throw water at the woman in the rainbow dress, but the woman had disappeared.

When her mother saw Francine returning home, she ran to meet her, cupping her hands in expectation. "Say something, my darling child, so that I can see your gift. Speak, speak."

"You are not going to like it, Mother," and with these words two toads and a snake fell from Francine's mouth into her mother's hands.

"Horrors!" screamed her mother, quickly dropping a snake. "What is all this?"

"Renée tricked us. It was not an old woman who asked for water, but a beautiful young lady," said Francine, spewing toads and snakes as she spoke.

"This is all Renée's fault," cried her mother. She reached for a broom and chased the poor girl out of the house. "Get out of my house and never come back," she shouted. She slammed the door shut and locked it.

Evening was coming, and Renée did not know where to go. Out of habit she took the path to the spring. There she sat on the rock and wondered what to do. She knew the village was nearby, but she had never been there. Only her stepsister and stepmother went to the village. But surely someone there must have work for her. She could cook, milk goats, and weed gardens. But it was too late to make any plans now, so she curled up and went to sleep.

Early in the morning she was awakened by the noise of hoofbeats. She looked up to see a young man who had stopped to water his horse. When he saw Renée, he asked, "What is a beautiful young girl doing here alone at this hour?"

Renée told him how her stepmother had driven her from the house and told her never to return. And with each word she spoke, a flower or a jewel fell from her lips. When the young man, who was the son of the king, questioned her about them, she told him everything that had happened.

The prince looked at her with kindness in his eyes and thought what a wonderful wife she would make. Though she did not come from a noble family, he felt she had a noble heart. And certainly his father, the king, would accept her spoken jewels as a dowry. He invited her to return to the palace with him.

Renée was so kind and gentle that soon everyone, including the king, loved her for herself rather than her jewels.

On the day of her wedding to the prince, as Renée spoke her marriage vows, neither jewels nor flowers fell from her lips, for now she no longer needed them.

Her sister, Francine, was not so fortunate. Even though her mother had forbidden her to speak, she continued to rant and rave. Soon the floor of their house was filled with hopping toads and slithering snakes. Finally her mother could stand it no longer, and she drove her daughter from the house. No one would take Francine in, so she found shelter in a cave in the forest and was never heard from again.

AUTHOR'S NOTE

Over nine hundred versions of the story-type identified as "The Kind and Unkind Sisters" have been recorded. It was one of the most popular of the early oral tales and was known throughout Europe in a number of forms. It has appeared in the Near East, Southern Asia, the Philippines, Japan, and Africa. Also, versions have been found in the Americas from Canada in the north to Chile in the south.

The story was well known in France prior to 1600. Over forty French versions have been recorded. It is not surprising, then, to find that Perrault included this particular story as one of five tales in his first manuscript version of 1695 that is now in the Pierpont Morgan Library in New York City. Perrault's title for this story was "The Fairies," and it appeared along with "The Sleeping Beauty," "Little Red Riding Hood," "Bluebeard," and "Puss-in-Boots." In his manuscript version the sisters were described as stepsisters. In the published version, *Histoires ou contes du temps passé* (1697), Perrault altered the relationship and made them sisters, probably to make the story less like "Cinderella," which was now included among the eight tales in this book.

While Perrault called the elder sister Franchon (or Fanny in English translations), he gave no name to the younger. I changed Franchon to Francine and named the younger Renée, which means reborn. I also tried to make Renée a resourceful character rather than the stereotypical helpless female of many fairy tales. The limitation placed upon the gifts was done simply because I felt that to speak flowers and jewels for the rest of your life would be a curse and not a gift. It also seemed important that Renée be accepted for her own true self.

Charlotte Huck   REDLANDS, CALIFORNIA

REFERENCES

Opie, Iona, and Peter Opie. *The Classic Fairy Tales*. London: Oxford University Press, 1974.

Perrault, Charles. *Histoires ou contes du temps passé*. Paris: Claude Barbin, 1698 (1st ed. 1697).

——. *Perrault's Tales of Mother Goose*. The dedication manuscript of 1695 reproduced in Collotype facsimile with introduction and critical text by Jacques Barchilon. New York: The Pierpont Morgan Library, 1956.

Philip, Neil, and Nicoletta Simborowski, translators. *The Complete Fairy Tales of Charles Perrault*. New York: Clarion Books, 1993.

Roberts, Warren E. *The Tale of the Kind and Unkind Girls*. Berlin: Walter de Gruyter and Company, 1958.